GARY AND GIBBY'S
SWIRLING, TWIRLING, WHIRLING WORRIES

By
Tina Rafowitz

PUBLISH HER

Wishing you a worry-free heart
Tina ♥

GARY AND GIBBY'S SWIRLING, TWIRLING, WHIRLING WORRIES

© Copyright 2024 Tina Rafowitz

All rights reserved. No portion of this book may be reproduced, stored in a retrieval system, or transmitted in any form or by any means—electronic, mechanical, photocopy, recording, scanning, or other—except for brief quotations in critical reviews or articles, without the prior written permission of the publisher.

Company and/or product names referenced in this book may be logos, trade names, trademarks, and/or registered trademarks, and are the property of their respective owners.

This book is not meant to be used, nor should it be used, to diagnose or treat any medical or psychological condition. Readers are advised to consult their own health care providers to determine the condition of, and best treatment for, the reader.

ISBN: 978-1-962457-02-6 (Softcover)
Printed in the United States of America
First Printing: 2024

Published by Publish Her, LLC
310 1/2 Main Street South
Stillwater, MN 55082
www.publishherpress.com

Written by Tina Rafowitz
Illustrated by Marty Harris

To my husband, Ivan,
and my children, Adam and Mia:
Your collective creativity constantly
inspires me.

And to Gibby:
You are always in our hearts.

TABLE OF CONTENTS

Last Day of Kindergarten............................1

The Surprise 9

Gibby's Gear 17

Goodnight Gibby 21

Lots to Learn 27

Storms and Scary Things 29

Puppy School 35

Play Dates 41

Vacation Adventure 45

First Day of First Grade 55

LAST DAY OF KINDERGARTEN

Gary's teacher, Mr. Wong,
tells the class the schedule
for the last day of kindergarten.
Gary likes to have a plan.
He does not like surprises.

Mr. Wong plays the piano
as the kids sing the morning song.
It is about sunshine and birds
and butterflies.

They practice letters and numbers.
Gary knows the alphabet.
He can sound out D-O-G,
M-O-M and D-A-D.
He can count all the way to 50.

For lunch, Gary's mom
always packs a sandwich,
wavy veggie chips
and a small orange.
Today he gets a cookie.
That's a good kind of surprise.

Gary gobs on sunscreen at recess.
His mind begins to whirl with worries.
He worries he will miss the ball
or fall when they play games.
He wishes he was as fast
as his friend Adam.

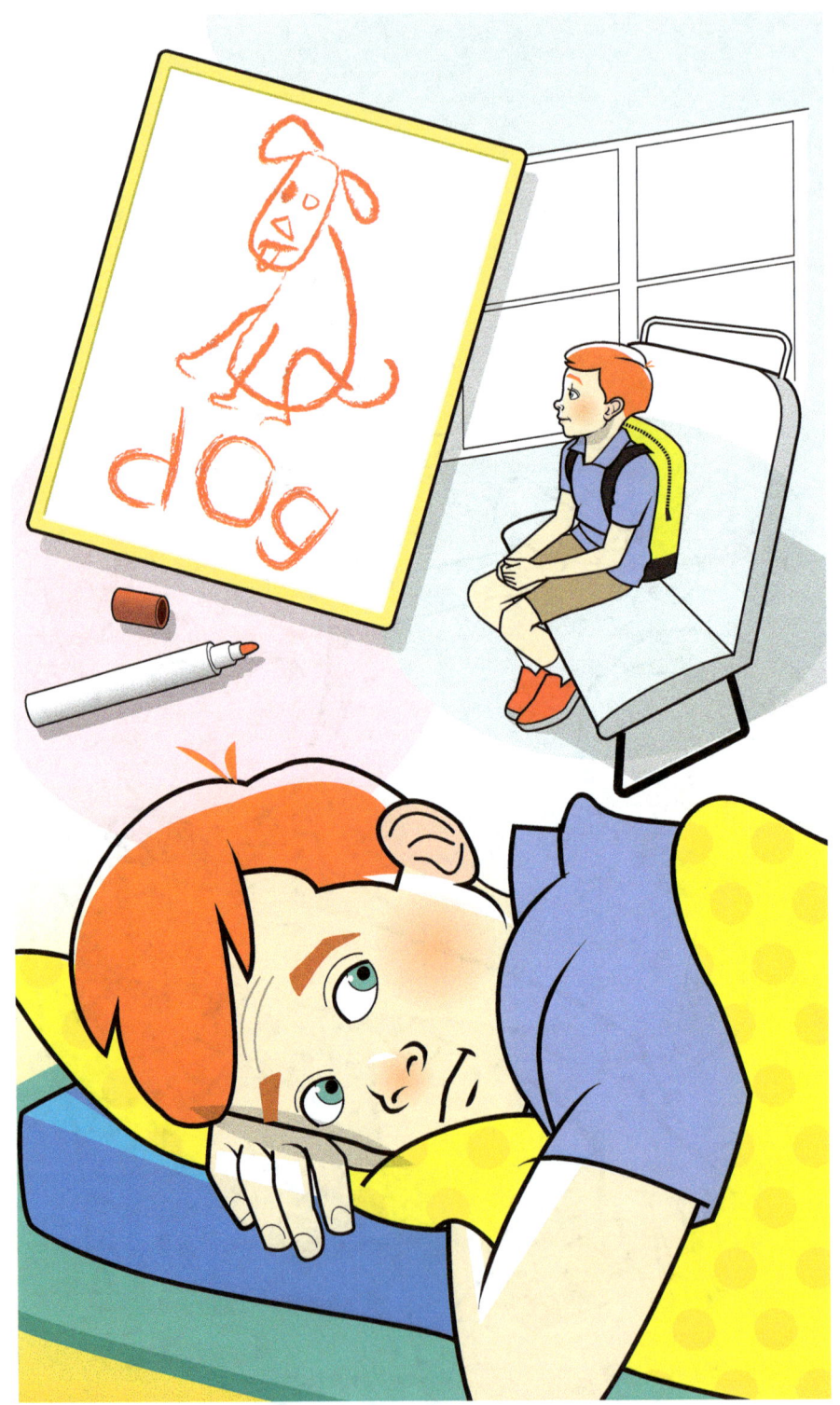

At rest time, Gary rolls out
his blue mat and lies down
under his fuzzy yellow blanket.
Mr. Wong turns on a machine
that makes calming sounds.
Gary's mind starts to swirl
and twirl and whirl with worries.

He worries about writing
neat letters on the board.

He worries the bus ride home
will be too noisy or bouncy.
"Will my friend Sara sit by me?"

He worries about whether
his mom or dad will be there
when he gets home from school.
"Will it be neighbor Nancy instead?"

Mostly he worries about summer.
He loves playing at the park
and swimming at the lake,
but change feels scary anyway.

Mom has been taking Gary
to a feelings doctor, Dr. Ivan.
He is helping Gary find ways
to worry less, but it is hard.

After resting, it is time for art.
When they are done,
they pack up all of their projects.
Gary wishes his art looked neat
like his friend Mia's.

At the end of the last day,
Gary waves goodbye
to his teacher and friends.
What surprises will summer bring?

THE SURPRISE

As the bus arrives at Gary's house,
both parents are outside with a box!
His eyes dart from Mom to Dad.
"Is something wrong?" he worries.

Mom usually works late
at her job as an accountant.
Dad is a high school music teacher.
He teaches jazz band after school.

His mom opens the box,
and something inside it is moving.
Gary opens his eyes wide.
That something is a furry black puppy!

Gary does not usually like surprises.
But he likes this one!
He rushes to meet his puppy.
He has wanted a pet
ever since his friend Sara got a cat.

His mom says, "They told us
this puppy is not very brave.
But we said, 'That's OK.
We will protect him.'
Gary, maybe you can help?"

Gary nods. "I will show him
what Dr. Ivan taught me to do
when I am worried or afraid.
And I will give him lots of hugs."

Gary sits on the grass
and Mom hands him the puppy.
He feels the puppy shiver and shake.
"It's OK, you are safe with me."

"He needs a name!" Gary exclaims.
"What if we call him Gibson?
Then both our names start with G.
It's also the name of Dad's guitar."
Dad thinks it is a very cool name.

Gibson has big dark eyes,
a furry black coat and brown paws.
They kind of look like mittens.

Mom explains that Gibson is a mix
of two kinds of dogs,
a poodle and a shih tzu.
"He's a shih-poo!" Mom says.
Gary laughs at that mix.

"I will call him Gibby for short," Gary says.

Gary thinks it is going to be the best summer ever.

GIBBY'S GEAR

Mom stays home with Gibby
while Gary and Dad go to the pet shop
to buy all the things a puppy needs.

Gary has been to this store before
with his friend Sara.
She invited him along to pick out
toys and treats for her cat.
Now it is Gary's turn to pick out
things for Gibby!

As they walk through the store,
Gary has an idea.
"Can we pick out gear that matches?"
he asks. "Everything black and white?"
Gary likes things that match.

"They may not have all the gear
we need in those colors," Dad says.
"But let's see what we can find."

Gary picks out:

1. A soft black-and-white striped bed.
2. A black-and-white checkered doggy carrier.
3. A crate with a cozy blue cushion for Gibby to sleep on.
4. A big bag of puppy food.
5. A bright red collar.

They drive home with all of
Gibby's new gear.
Gary thinks of something important
he learned from Dr. Ivan.
"We need a schedule for Gibby.
A schedule helps me worry less."

"That's a great idea," says Dad.
"What will we put on Gibby's schedule?"

Gary thinks for a minute and says,
"When he should eat and go potty
and take a walk.
And when it's time to sleep in his crate."

Dad says Gibby will feel safe in the crate.
It will also teach him not to go potty
in the house or chew on things.
Gibby has everything he needs
to feel at home at Gary's house.

GOODNIGHT GIBBY

Soon it is dinnertime for Gibby.
He eats all of his puppy food.
Then Gary takes him to a special spot
in the backyard to poop and potty.

It has been a big day and Gary is tired.
"I think Gibby should go to bed
when I go to bed," he says.
"Can we put his crate in my room?"

"Let's try it," both parents agree.
They settle Gibby in the crate
on the floor next to Gary's bed.
Gibby has a yellow stuffed rabbit.

Gary lies down in his own cozy bed.
Suddenly he realizes something!
His mind has not swirled or twirled
or whirled with too many worries today.

Just when Gary's eyes feel sleepy,
Gibby begins to whimper loudly.
Mom rushes in and says,
"Maybe we should move his crate
out of your room."

"No, Mom, it's OK," Gary says.
"Please let him stay here."

"We can give it another try," Mom says.

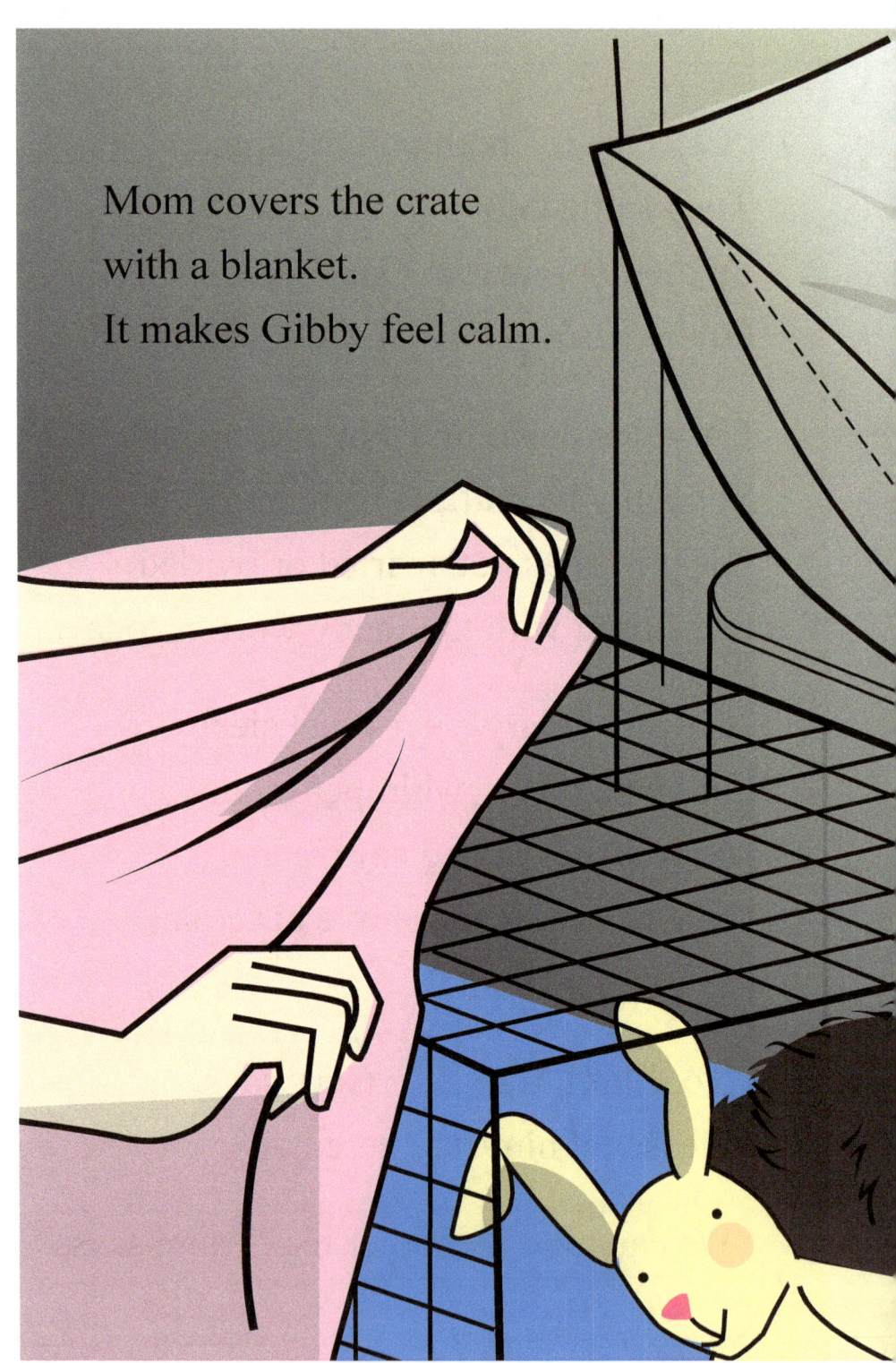

Mom covers the crate
with a blanket.
It makes Gibby feel calm.

Gibby quiets down
and they both fall asleep,
snug, safe and sound.

LOTS TO LEARN

The next day, Gibby howls at 6 a.m.
Gary's eyes pop open.
"This is not on the schedule," Gary says.
"You are supposed to wake up at 7 a.m.
and go outside to potty."

"I will take him outside," Mom says.

Gary hopes Gibby will learn his
schedule soon.
He calls Sara and she comes over.
Gibby runs to greet her.
Sara is very gentle with Gibby.
She sits on the ground and pets him.

Gary's backyard has a fence
so they play outside.
Gibby sniffs the grass and flowers.
He even chases a squirrel.

Sara stays for lunch.
They eat pepperoni pizza!
Gibby takes a nap in his crate.
He is a tired puppy!

Gibby has a few potty accidents.
First on Mom's favorite rug.
And later on the kitchen floor.
Mom and Dad remind Gary
to keep an eye on Gibby
whenever he is not in his crate.

There is a lot to teach a puppy.
Gary firmly says "off"
when Gibby starts to chew
on the wrong things.
The training book is teaching
them both new things.

STORMS AND SCARY THINGS

Gary does not like storms.
A little rain is OK.
But not the scary flashes of lightning.
And not the loud cracks of thunder.

The first big summer storm rolls in.
Gibby does not like storms either.
Not one bit!
His eyes get all buggy
and he shakes and pants.

Gary holds and hugs Gibby gently.
"It's going to be OK," he says.
"The rain will water the grass
and the flowers and the trees."
But Gibby still shakes.

"I have an idea, Mom!" Gary says.
"Remember my heavy blanket
that makes me feel calmer?
Maybe if I wrap Gibby in his blanket,
he will not shake."

Gibby calms down in his blanket.
Mom says they will get him
a ThunderShirt, a snug jacket
that makes dogs feel safe.

The house is quiet again.
Gary realizes he did not worry
about his own fears during the storm.
He was too busy helping Gibby!

Gary soon finds out
that Gibby has a lot of fears.
Like riding in the car.
And going to the vet.

And meeting new dogs.
And big, loud trucks.
Dr. Ivan helps Gary understand
his many fears.
Now Gary helps Gibby, too.

PUPPY SCHOOL

Gary and Gibby go to puppy school
when Gibby is 12 weeks old.
Gary feels scared in new groups.
His head swirls and twirls and whirls
with worries.

He worries about being the smallest kid.
He worries that he sweats a lot.
He worries about his lisp.
He worries Gibby will be scared, too.

"You are a smart puppy," Gary says.
"You have soft fur and kind eyes.
I hope you can make one new friend."

It works! A dog with reddish-brown fur
and long ears walks over to sniff Gibby.
He is not shaky or scared.
Soon the puppies chase each other.

The teacher's name is Ms. Katie.
She teaches a lot of puppy facts.
Gary is not listening too well.
He is busy watching Gibby
play with the long-eared dog.

The smaller dogs are put in one group.
The bigger dogs go in another group.
Gary thinks the teachers at school
should do this with kids, too.

A tall boy with dark hair and glasses
picks up the dog with the long ears.
"My name is Kevin," the boy says.
"This is my dog, Willy."

Gary learns Kevin will be in
second grade next year.
He likes to cook with his mom.
And he listens to jazz music with his dad.

"Shush!" Ms. Katie says to the boys. They stop talking while she teaches, and try to pay attention.

PLAY DATES

The boys plan a play date.
Kevin lives in an apartment,
so Gary invites him and Willy over.
The puppies run and play together.
The boys laugh and talk.

"It's cool that both our dads
like jazz music," Gary says.
The new friends have a lot in common.

When Gary and Kevin meet up again,
they take the puppies on a walk.
Their moms follow close behind.

CRASH! BOOM! BEEP-BEEP-BEEP!

"Oh no!" Gary shouts over the noise.
"It's Monday! Garbage day!"
The garbage trucks are too loud.
Gibby is shaking.

"Dr. Ivan told me it's OK to say no
if something feels wrong," Gary says.
It's clear that a walk on garbage day
feels wrong to Gibby.
They plan a walk for Tuesday instead.

It is almost the end of summer.
School begins in two weeks.
Gary and Gibby have helped each other
through so many worries!

VACATION ADVENTURE

Mom and Dad have another surprise!
The family is going to visit
Grandma and Grandpa in Florida.
One more adventure before school starts!

"Can I bring Gibby on the airplane?"
Gary asks his parents.
They nod and Gary shouts "Yippee!"

They find their seats on the airplane.
Gibby huddles in his doggy carrier.
Then Gary places Gibby
under the seat for takeoff.

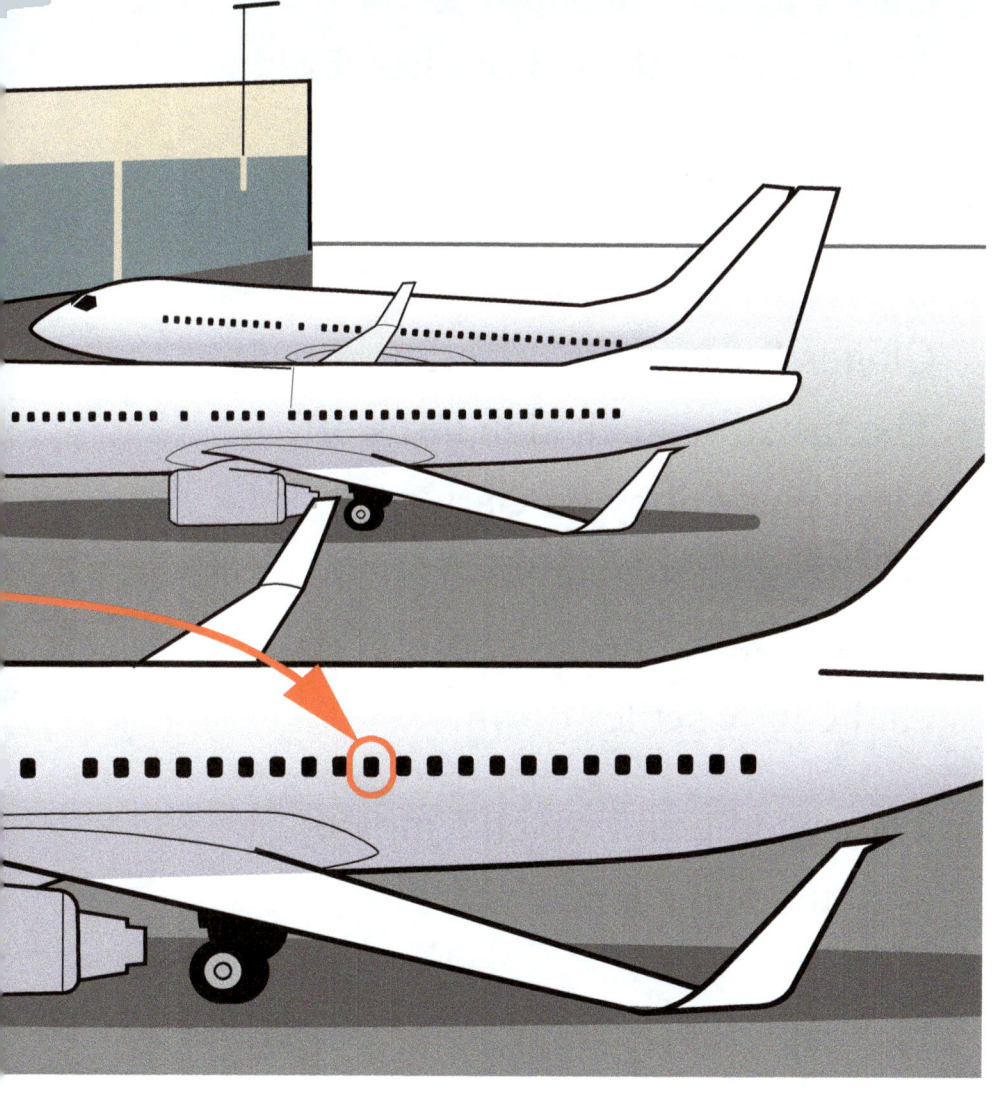

The jet engine roars to life.
Gibby's eyes get very wide,
and he shakes and cries.
Gary can feel his puppy's fear.
He wants to help and reaches for him.

"Not until the plane takes off,"
Mom reminds him.

Clouds float past the window.
The fasten seatbelt sign turns off.
Mom puts Gibby on Gary's lap.
Gary hugs him gently.
"You're safe," he says softly.
And Gibby settles down.

They cuddle and watch a movie
until the plane lands.

They stay at Grandma and Grandpa's
apartment near the beach.
The ocean water is warm.
Gibby is afraid of the waves.
He chases bubbles and birds instead.

Later they go to a fancy restaurant
with cloth napkins and extra forks.
The kind that does NOT allow dogs.
Gibby stays in Grandma's bathroom
so he feels safe while they are gone.

The fancy dinner takes a long time.
Gary can't stop thinking about Gibby.
His tummy aches and his head swirls
and twirls and whirls with worry.

When they finally get home,
Grandma's neighbor is angry.
She says Gibby cried loudly
the whole time they were gone.

The very next day,
Grandma buys Gibby a doggy stroller.
Now they take him everywhere.
For the rest of the vacation!

Soon their vacation is over.
They had a fun time in Florida.
Gary hugs Grandma and Grandpa
and tells them goodbye.

The airplane ride home is bumpy.
It feels like they are driving
on a rocky road in the sky.
The plane teeters and totters.

They pass through fluffy clouds,
and the sky is blue again.
The airplane stops bouncing,
and Gary and Gibby fall asleep.

When the plane lands,
they are happy to be back home.
Gary is proud of Gibby,
and he is proud of himself.
They tried many new things.

FIRST DAY OF FIRST GRADE

It is the first day of first grade!
Gary frowns and his mind whirls.
He is worried about leaving Gibby.

"He will be OK," says Dad.
"Neighbor Nancy will check on him twice a day."

Kevin goes to a different school.
But Sara will be on Gary's bus.

The school bus stops at Gary's corner.
Gary gives Gibby a new chew toy,
and hugs him goodbye.
"See you real soon," Gary says.

He wipes the tears from his eyes.
He spots Sara through the window.
They sit together on the bus,
and share their favorite summer stories.

"I went to my cousin's farm," says Sara.
"I saw baby goats and piglets!"

"I went to Florida to visit
my grandma and grandpa," says Gary.
"And Gibby got to come along!"

They are excited to start first grade,
and meet their new teacher, Ms. Oliver.

The bus turns the final corner.
Ms. Oliver is in front of the school.
She is holding a big sign that says
"Welcome to first grade."
Gary can read all those words.

Gary sees some of his friends
from kindergarten last year.
Like Adam! And Mia!
His mind is not swirling or twirling
or whirling with worries.

A smile spreads over Gary's face.
He feels something new.
He feels excited!

He is excited to meet new kids.
He is excited to see his new schedule.
He is excited to tell the class
about his great summer with Gibby.

And he is excited to see Gibby later to share all about first grade.

THE END

RESOURCES

Additional resources for children who worry and the adults who care for them:

- "Anxiety-Free Kids" by Bonnie Zucker
- "Breaking Free of Child Anxiety and OCD: A Scientifically Proven Program for Parents" by Eli R. Lebowitz
- "Helping Your Anxious Child" by Ronald Rapee, et al.
- American Academy of Child and Adolescent Psychiatry (www.aacap.org)
- Anxiety and Depression Association of America (www.aada.org)
- National Institute of Mental Health (www.nimh.nih.gov)

ACKNOWLEDGMENTS

Thanks to Chris Olsen and the Publish Her team. You made the publishing process both effortless and fun. Thanks to Molly Beth Griffin for original edits. Special thanks to my family and friends for your support and encouragement.

ABOUT THE AUTHOR

Minnesota-based author Tina Rafowitz is a retired accountant and recruiter with a passion for family, travel and entertaining. After raising two kids and a shih-poo with separation anxiety, Tina found herself with an empty nest and a mind brimming with ideas. She honed her narrative voice through creative nonfiction, and developed a distinct writing flair that is unapologetically Tina.

Tina writes about everything from her neurotic dog, Gibby, to her travel adventures. Her work has been published in "Chicken Soup for the Soul: 101 Tales of Canine Companionship" and in Wanderlust Journal. She also published a cookbook called "Tina's Table." "Gary and Gibby's Swirling, Twirling, Whirling Worries" is Tina's first children's book.

For more information, and to read Tina's latest works, visit www.tinacharlesrafowitz.com.

ABOUT PUBLISH HER

Publish Her is a female-founded independent publisher dedicated to elevating the words, writing and stories of women. We are passionate about amplifying the voices of women of color, women with disabilities and members of the LGBTQ+ community, and we aim to make publishing an attainable, exciting and collaborative process for all. To learn more, visit www.publishherpress.com.

Printed in the USA
CPSIA information can be obtained
at www.ICGtesting.com
LVHW021035090824
787663LV00001B/2